Aliens Don't Carve Jack-o'-lanterns

Want more Bailey School Kids?
Check these out!

 #1-46

SUPER SPECIALS #1- 6

 #1-9

And don't miss the...

HOLIDAY SPECIALS

Swamp Monsters Don't Chase Wild Turkeys

Aliens Don't Carve Jack-o'-lanterns

Coming soon...

Mrs. Claus Doesn't Climb Telephone Poles

Aliens Don't Carve Jack-o'-lanterns

by Debbie Dadey
and
Marcia Thornton Jones

illustrated by John Steven Gurney

A
LITTLE APPLE
PAPERBACK

SCHOLASTIC INC.
New York   Toronto   London   Auckland   Sydney
Mexico City   New Delhi   Hong Kong   Buenos Aires

To Patrick Winters
— DD

To Steve — for carving the best
jack-o'-lanterns on this, and all other, planets!
— MTJ

ISBN 0-439-40831-8

12 11 10 9 8 7 6 5 4 3 2 1   2 3 4 5 6 7/0

Printed in the U.S.A.   40
First Scholastic printing, September 2002

Contents

1

Gotcha!

"Trick or treat. Smell my feet. Give me something good to eat. If you don't, I don't care. 'Cause I can see your underwear," Eddie sang.

His friend Liza giggled. "Eddie," she said. "It's still a whole week before Halloween. It's too early for trick-or-treating."

Eddie and Liza were waiting for their friends under the playground's oak tree so that they could all walk into school together. If there was one thing Eddie was not good at, it was waiting.

"It's never too early for a few good tricks," he said. Suddenly, Eddie's eyes grew big and he pointed toward Liza's belly button. "Look at the size of that spider!"

When Liza squealed and looked down, Eddie bonked her on the nose with his finger. "Gotcha!" he said.

Liza put her hands on her hips and leaned close to Eddie. "You won't get any treats on Halloween if you aren't nice," she warned.

Eddie hopped up and grabbed a tree branch as Howie and Melody jogged across the playground. "Halloween is the best time of year," Eddie yelled to the highest branch of the tree. "I can't wait to get candy."

"For once, I agree with Eddie," Howie said as he and Melody crunched through the leaves toward their friends. "I'm looking forward to getting candy, too. Chocolate is the best! I hope I get lots of candy bars."

Eddie jumped down from the tree and looked past Melody. "Watch out!" he yelled.

Melody ducked so fast she fell to the

ground. When she did, Eddie laughed out loud. "Gotcha!" he said.

Melody did not look happy. She stood up and brushed leaves from the knees of her jeans. "You're the one that better watch out!"

Eddie grinned. "Don't get mad. I'm just practicing my tricks for Halloween. Why does Halloween have to be at the *end* of October?" he complained. "Why is it only once a year?"

Howie laughed. "I don't think Bailey City could survive Eddie's tricks if they happened more than once a year."

Melody dropped her blue backpack on the ground. "I'm glad it's only once a year and a whole week away," she said. "Coming up with the perfect costume is hard work."

"Work, smerk," Eddie grumbled. "I don't have time for work. I'm too busy practicing my tricks."

"Working on your costume is half the fun of Halloween," Liza argued.

"Then my grandmother is having fun," Eddie told her, "because she's making my costume for me."

Melody shook her head. "You should at least help your grandmother," she said. "My alien costume is going to be so cool. I'm painting a control panel on the front and I'm using wires to make my hair stand up like antennae." Melody held up her black braids to show her friends what they would look like.

The grin on Eddie's face slipped into a frown. "An alien does sound great. My grandmother doesn't know anything about spacemen. She said the only thing she could make was a silly Viking costume."

Melody patted Eddie on the shoulder. "There's nothing silly about Vikings. They were brave adventurers and warriors. Remember when we studied Erik the Red?"

"That's right," Liza said. "We can call you Eddie the Terrible!"

Liza and Melody giggled, but Howie didn't. "I wouldn't mind being a Viking," he said. "Or an alien. I have to wear an old cowboy suit my dad had."

"You'll never guess what I'm going to be," Liza said.

"Sleeping Beauty?" Melody guessed.

"A scientist?" Howie asked.

"A wart-covered toad?" Eddie joked.

Liza shook her head so hard her blonde ponytail whipped around. "My costume will be the most original of all," she said. "I'm going to be the Statue of Liberty, a great symbol of our country's freedom!"

"That sounds great," Melody said.

"Sounds weird to me," Eddie teased. "Hey, take a look at that guy. He looks like he's already dressed up for Halloween."

"Don't look," Liza warned. "This sounds like one of Eddie's 'gotcha' pranks."

"I'm serious this time," Eddie told them.

6

"We're not falling for it," Howie said with a shake of his head.

Eddie jumped up and down and pointed toward the school. "Believe me! This guy is out of this world."

Melody shook her head, too. "You can't trick me twice. You know what they say? Fool me once, shame on you, fool me twice, shame on me!"

"You have to look or it'll be too late," Eddie yelled. Before Howie and Liza could say another word, Eddie grabbed their arms and twirled them around.

2

Stranger Than Most

Liza, Melody, Howie, and Eddie watched a very short man trot up the steps to Bailey Elementary School. Dried leaves swirled around his silver boots.

"That man looks like he's eaten too much candy already," Eddie said.

Liza shook her finger in front of Eddie's nose. "It's not nice to make fun of people," she warned. "You can't help it that you were born with freckles and that man can't help it that he's a little short and round."

"But he could help the way he dresses," Eddie pointed out.

"There's nothing wrong with what he's wearing," Melody said slowly.

"Most people don't wear shiny silver

9

shirts with sparkling buttons," Howie told her.

The shirt wasn't the only shiny thing the stranger wore. He also had on blue pants that reflected cars from the parking lot. His hair stuck up in two points on top of his head.

"The way his hair sticks up makes him look like a giant caterpillar with antennae," Melody said.

"Why would he be going into our school?" Eddie wondered out loud.

"Maybe we should tell Principal Davis," Liza suggested. "Strangers aren't supposed to wander around the school."

"And that man," Eddie said as he pulled his ball cap down over his red hair, "is definitely stranger than most."

"I'm sure we have nothing to worry about," Melody told her friends. "Visitors have to sign in at the main office."

Howie nodded. "We can make sure he doesn't get lost."

The kids headed into the building. They

followed the stranger down the darkened halls of Bailey Elementary. The stranger walked as if he was on a mission. He didn't stop to look at the paintings of pumpkins, the leaf print posters, or even the haunted house murals. In fact, the man didn't look in any direction except straight ahead, and he didn't stop until he reached the main office.

The kids peeked through the window after the stranger went inside. Principal Davis was busy in his office. The secretary was nowhere to be seen.

The stranger headed toward Principal Davis's office. He stopped suddenly, and slowly turned toward the secretary's desk.

Liza smiled. "He must have realized he needs to sign the Visitors' Log." But Liza was wrong. Instead of signing the Visitors' Log, the stranger opened the candy jar on the secretary's desk and scooped out a handful of chocolate. Then he stuffed it all into his mouth.

"No fair," Eddie yelped. "That candy is for kids when they're good."

Liza giggled. "Then it doesn't matter to you because you'll never get any of that candy anyway!"

3

Big Surprise

In their classroom, Eddie was the first to tell their teacher about the strange man that sneaked into the building and stole the secretary's chocolate. "It's not fair," he added. "That chocolate is for kids."

Mrs. Jeepers gently touched the brooch at her throat with a finger tipped in green nail polish. It was no secret that most third-graders suspected Mrs. Jeepers was a vampire and the pin she always wore had the power to make kids behave. "Good students," she added, "are allowed a treat from the chocolate jar if they work hard."

Eddie slumped in his chair. He hated the way teachers always talked about working when all he wanted to do was play.

"Do not be alarmed," Mrs. Jeepers told the rest of the class. "The stranger Eddie speaks of is welcome at Bailey Elementary School. In fact, he is planning a big surprise for all of us."

"Surprise?" Eddie said, sitting back up. "I like surprises. Especially when they're covered with chocolate."

Mrs. Jeepers smiled her odd little half smile. "Mr. Spark is a professional party planner," she explained. "There is to be a Halloween party at our school on the Saturday before Halloween. Students are invited to help decorate after school today."

All of the kids clapped except for Eddie. He slumped back down in his seat. "That sounds like more work to me," he groaned.

After school, Eddie, Melody, Liza, and Howie met in their usual spot. A brisk

breeze tore leaves loose from the oak tree, and they settled on the ground next to the kids' sneakers. Eddie pulled his baseball cap down over his red hair to block the cool wind.

"This will be great," Melody said. "We already get to go to the mall for trick-or-treating and now there's a Halloween party. We'll get to celebrate two times instead of one."

"Does that mean we get twice the candy?" Eddie asked.

"The party will be better than a bag full of candy," Liza added. "And even more fun than trick-or-treating because we get to play games."

"But what about candy?" Eddie asked. "You can never have enough candy."

Howie put his hand on Eddie's arm. "Forget about candy for now. Mrs. Jeepers didn't give us any homework, so that we could help in the gym. We'd better get in there."

Eddie kicked at a leaf. "Working after

17

school isn't my idea of fun. I'd rather sneak in and raid the secretary's chocolate jar."

"You don't get candy unless you help," Liza reminded him.

"So, unless you want to eat spinach for Halloween, you better get busy!" Melody said with a giggle.

"Last one there is a rotten egg!" Eddie yelled as he took off running.

"Too late," Liza yelled as she and her two friends raced after him. "You're already the biggest rotten egg in Bailey City!"

Eddie was out of breath when he reached the gym door. "Hanging streamers will be easy," Eddie said as he pulled open the big metal door.

Howie, Melody, and Liza crowded behind Eddie to look inside.

"What happened to our gym?" Liza squealed.

4

The Planet Liron

The gym had been transformed into a scene from an outer space movie. Shiny silver paper covered the walls, bright green and orange control panels lined the room. Silver stars and planets twinkled from the ceiling.

Several other third-graders clustered around the man in shiny pants.

"We are going to have a ball at the party," Mr. Spark was saying as Melody, Liza, Howie, and Eddie made their way toward the group of kids. Mr. Spark spoke faster and faster as he told the kids his plans. "I've studied the history of your Halloween celebration and I have planned the perfect party. First, there will be a costume contest. I'm sure there will

be many Martians, space bugs, and Mytok invaders. Then we'll bob for apples."

A girl named Carey raised her hand. "I can't get my golden curls wet," she said.

Mr. Spark looked worried. "Will they fall off?" he asked.

Carey giggled. Once she assured him her hair was real and would not come off in the water, Mr. Spark continued telling the kids about his plans for the party.

"After we bob for apples, I will be your DJ for the Halloween dance. I'm picking out all the traditional favorites like 'Monster Mash,' 'Purple People Eater,' and 'Night on Bald Mountain.'"

"Is that a song about Principal Davis's bald head?" Eddie asked in his most innocent voice.

Liza jabbed Eddie in the side. "You'll get in trouble for making fun of the principal," she warned.

Mr. Spark didn't seem mad. In fact, he looked confused. "I do not believe your principal's head is the same thing as a mountain," Mr. Spark said slowly before continuing to tell them what he had planned for the party. "The evening will end with a pumpkin-decorating contest. I've even been practicing. I carved my jack-o'-lanterns. You will use markers and paint for yours."

Mr. Spark hurried to the side of the stage to pull a heavy cord. Slowly, the blood-red stage curtains squeaked open. There, lined up on the stage, were eight jack-o'-lanterns. Only these jack-o'-lanterns didn't look like most. One had three eyes. Another had four noses. A third had eight antennae stuck on with poster putty.

"Aren't they wonderful?" Mr. Spark asked. "You will get to decorate your own creations Saturday night at the party. The most creative pumpkin wins a surprise!"

Eddie pushed to the front of the kids. "I don't care about apples. I don't care

about jack-o'-lanterns. I definitely don't care about dancing. What I want to know is when we get to fill our treat bags with creamy, gooey chocolate."

"Yeah," a boy named Huey echoed. "When do we get the candy?"

The smile seemed to slide right off Mr. Spark's face. "This party will feature a different type of trick-or-treating," he told them, suddenly very serious. "When you come to the party you must all BRING a bag of candy."

Then he clapped his hands three times. "Enough chit-chat," he hollered. "Let's get busy, busy, BUSY!"

Most of the kids hurried to follow Mr. Spark's directions. Not Eddie. His face was red and he threw his baseball cap on the ground next to Howie's sneakers. "What planet is this guy from?" Eddie muttered. "Everyone knows you GET candy at Halloween. You don't GIVE candy!"

Liza stared at Eddie. "What did you just say?"

Eddie didn't answer her because Mr. Spark interrupted them. "Work, work, work," he yelled. "We must have the gym ready for Saturday night!"

Melody stepped up. "I'll hang orange and black streamers from the bleachers," she suggested.

"No, no, no," Mr. Spark yelped. "That will never do. Everything must look exactly like the planet Liron," he stressed.

"Liron?" Howie asked. "I've never heard of that planet."

"It's from another solar system, far away from here," Mr. Spark explained. "Now, I need you four to stuff tiny bits of paper into this wire screen to make it look like a giant Plybton."

"Plybton?" Howie blurted. "What's that?"

Mr. Spark paused long enough to put his hands on his hips and peer down at

Howie. "You ask a lot of questions," he muttered. "And I have no time to answer them all. Now, let's get to work, work, WORK!"

The kids stuffed tissue paper into a wire screen like Mr. Spark told them, but Eddie quickly lost interest. Goofing off was his plan. He wandered over and started pushing buttons on one of the control panels. A loud whir erupted in the gym and the lights flashed on and off.

"Eddie," Liza squealed as the lights flashed one last time and a siren went off. "What have you done?"

5

End of the World

"I thought Mr. Spark was going to bite off Eddie's head," Howie told his friends as they walked home.

"That would never happen," Liza said seriously. "Eddie isn't sweet enough."

Eddie took off his hat and thumped Liza on the head with it. "It wasn't my fault the circuit breaker blew," Eddie said, squishing down his red hair as he pushed the cap back on.

"Mr. Spark thought it was," Melody said. "Did you see his eyes? He was so mad they glowed green!"

"I hope he cools down in time for Saturday's party," Liza said. "It would be a shame if Eddie didn't get to come."

Howie nodded. "I'm sure Mr. Spark

was kidding about the candy. I bet there will be tons of sweets at the party. Especially since we all have to bring a bag."

"Nothing can keep me away," Eddie bragged. "I'd do anything for candy. I'd even battle a three-headed monster from outer space."

"You're worse than any monster I know," Howie said with a laugh.

On their way home, Eddie pulled his friends into the small market on the corner.

"Why are we going in here?" Liza wanted to know.

Eddie's stomach rumbled. "Because, all this talk about a Halloween party made me realize how hungry I am. I want to look at all the candy I plan to get trick-or-treating." Eddie started counting out candies on his fingers. "Caramels, licorice, and most of all, chocolate."

Liza smiled. "I guess looking won't hurt."

"Too bad we don't have any money," Howie said. "We could buy a snack right now."

Melody giggled. "I have two whole dollars in my pocket. I could treat you."

Eddie felt like hugging Melody. Instead, he hurried down the aisles of the store. But when they reached the section where the candy was kept, they screeched to a halt.

"What happened?" Melody asked.

"It's the end of the world," Eddie groaned, his hands holding his cheeks.

"There must be a simple and logical explanation," Howie said slowly.

The four kids stared at the shelves. There wasn't a piece of candy in sight. The shelves were totally empty.

"Howie is right," Liza said. "Everyone must have bought all the candy for Halloween. I'm sure the store will order more."

"They'd better," Eddie said, holding up a fist. "Or I'll send them to the moon!"

Liza stumbled back against a bread display. Eight bags tumbled to the floor, but Liza didn't notice.

"What's wrong?" Eddie asked Liza. "Did your legs stop working?"

Liza shook her head. Her eyes were wide open. She opened her mouth, but no words came out.

6

Invasion From
Outer Space

Melody rushed to Liza's side and thumped her on the back. Liza gasped. She swallowed. She blinked.

"Are you okay?" Howie asked.

Liza looked each of her friends in the eyes. Finally, she shook her head. "No, I'm not okay. And neither are you. In fact, Bailey City is in serious trouble!"

"I agree," Eddie said. "There isn't a single piece of candy to be found and Halloween is only a few days away. What could be worse than that?"

"I'll tell you what's worse," Liza said. "Mr. Spark is an alien from the planet Liron!"

"What?" Melody, Howie, and Eddie blurted out at once.

33

"It's as obvious as two plus two," Liza said, pulling her friends close so no one else could hear what she told them. "He appears out of nowhere. His clothes are as shiny as a spacesuit, and he's turning our gym into a planet that no one has ever heard of before. What if we're really helping an alien instead of planning a party?"

Melody didn't believe Liza for one second. "There are no such things as aliens from outer space," Melody pointed out.

Howie stepped up. Howie knew everything there was to know about space because his dad worked at the Federal Aeronautics Technology Station, otherwise known as FATS.

"Actually," Howie said in his most scientific voice, "the possibility of the existence of life forms living on other planets has not been disproved. After all, there is a lot of space. Why would life only exist on one tiny speck of a planet?"

Eddie glared at Howie. "Stop talking

like an encyclopedia and say that in plain English," Eddie told Howie.

"What Howie is saying," Liza said, "is that somewhere out there in space, there is probably at least one other planet with aliens living on it. I believe that planet is Liron and Mr. Spark is getting ready to invade Bailey City!"

Melody sighed. "Even if there were aliens, why would they come to Bailey City?"

Howie held up his hand and started ticking off reasons. "To take over our planet; to hide from bad aliens; to learn about humans. To get something they don't have on their own planet."

"Or," Eddie interrupted, "to trick-or-treat and steal all our candy!"

Liza didn't laugh along with Eddie. She was serious. Dead serious. "I think Eddie is right," she gasped and pointed to the empty candy shelves. "I think Mr. Spark is an alien and he's here to steal all our candy — especially the chocolate!"

Melody giggled. Howie smiled. Eddie laughed out loud. "I doubt an alien would zoom across space for light-years just because he has a sweet tooth," Eddie said.

Liza shook her head. "Don't you get it? Everyone knows that candy gives kids energy."

"That's true," Eddie said. "That's why my grandmother won't let me have any candy at night."

"What if," Liza said slowly, "aliens from Liron have learned to use the energy from candy to power spaceships?"

"That would mean Mr. Spark would need all the candy he can find," Howie said slowly.

"Exactly," Liza said. "When he's drained all the candy from Bailey City, he'll go to other cities. He and his invading aliens won't leave our planet until there isn't a piece of candy left anywhere on Earth!"

7

Little Green Men
and Mummies

"I don't believe in aliens, but if they do exist I'm pretty sure they don't plan parties and they definitely don't carve jack-o'-lanterns," Melody told Liza. "I'm not listening to your bunch of baloney anymore. Your tall tales of little green men from outer space aren't going to ruin my Halloween fun."

The next day after school, Melody went to the gym. She wanted to help get it in shape for the Halloween party, even if Mr. Spark didn't like her ideas. Liza and Howie dragged Eddie with them. Eddie wasn't interested in helping. He wanted to goof off, but Mr. Spark didn't give him a chance.

"Please finish this Plybton right away,"

Mr. Spark directed the kids, handing them more bright yellow tissue paper to stuff into a wire screen.

"I wonder what a Plybton is," Melody said as Mr. Spark walked away.

"It's probably a big snake that sucks all the snot out of your body," Eddie teased Melody.

Liza giggled and put tissue paper on her head. "Maybe a Plybton is a giant chicken that lays chocolate eggs."

"MMMM, that's my kind of chicken." Howie laughed.

Eddie grabbed a big wad of streamers and wrapped them around himself. "Roar," Eddie bellowed. "Guess what I am?"

"A rotten banana?" Howie asked.

"Very funny," Eddie snapped. "I'm a Plybton mummy."

Melody shook her head. "Eddie, you better stop goofing off before Mr. Spark sees you."

Eddie couldn't stop. He was too excited.

He took tissue paper and stuffed it down his shirt. "Look, I'm a Plybton warthog."

Liza giggled so Eddie grabbed a big wad of paper and held it on his backside. "Gobble, gobble," Eddie clucked. "I'm a Plybton turkey."

Melody rolled her eyes. "You're a turkey all right. Quit acting silly before . . ."

"Uh-oh," Liza said. "Too late." She gulped as Mr. Spark headed their way.

"You're in for it now," Howie warned. "I hope Mr. Spark doesn't like turkey as a snack."

Melody gulped. "Look at his eyes." Sure enough, Mr. Spark's eyes glowed green.

"We'd better get out of here before it's too late," Howie whispered.

"Wait," Melody said. "Maybe he didn't see Eddie after all." Instead of marching over to the kids, Mr. Spark stepped behind the stage curtain.

"Whew," Liza said. "I thought you were a goner."

Suddenly the lights went out, and sev-

eral kids screamed. In just a few minutes the lights came back on.

"Wow," Howie said. "It's as dark as outer space in here when the lights go out."

"That was scary," Melody admitted, dropping her tissue paper. "Thank goodness everyone is all right."

Howie slowly shook his head. "Everyone isn't all right. Eddie and Liza have disappeared!"

8

Blast Off

"What if Liza was right about Mr. Spark," Melody gasped, "and he really is an alien? What if he took Liza and Eddie back to the planet Liron with him?"

Howie's face grew very pale. "We better find Liza and Eddie and make sure they're okay."

Melody and Howie sneaked behind the heavy blood-red stage curtain. Mr. Spark's back was to them so they quickly went down a side hallway. The only light came from an exit sign that glowed eerily in the darkness. "Maybe this isn't such a good idea," Melody whispered.

Howie didn't look so sure either. "This better not be one of Eddie's 'gotcha' tricks," Howie said. "Because it isn't funny."

The kids tiptoed down the tiny hallway. Even though they were trying to be quiet, their footsteps echoed like thunder. Strange props from old plays hung on the walls of the hallway. Howie and Melody passed big masks, a king's costume, and fake trees. Melody grabbed Howie when a plastic skeleton swung out in front of them.

"If we don't find them in two minutes," Melody said with a shudder, "I'm getting out of here and telling Mrs. Jeepers so she can help us look."

Howie knew Melody wasn't serious. After all, they both thought that their teacher, Mrs. Jeepers, was a vampire. They didn't really want to search in the dark with a vampire teacher.

Howie pointed to an open door. "Let's check in there." A green glow lit up the entire backstage room. As soon as Howie and Melody walked inside the room, they glowed green, too.

Melody giggled nervously. "You really do look like one of Liza's little green men."

"What is that thing?" Howie said. "I've never seen anything like it." Both kids stared at a large green blob that sat in the middle of the room. It looked like an upside-down bowl of lime Jell-O, except one hundred times bigger.

"It glows just like Mr. Spark's eyes," Melody said with a gulp. "You don't think it's alive, do you?"

Howie shook his head and tried to be brave. "I'm sure that's just something for the Halloween party."

Melody nodded and scooted around the green blob. "This party is getting weirder and weirder," she said. "Look at that." She pointed to a big electrical panel. Levers, knobs, and buttons glowed in every color of the rainbow. One button flashed on and off. The button said BLAST OFF.

"Something about this isn't right,"

Howie said. "That looks like the kind of control panel my dad works with at the Federal Aeronautics Technology Station."

"I don't care about that. I just want to know what happened to Liza and Eddie," Melody said.

Howie's face glowed green, but he still looked very serious when he told Melody, "I'm afraid we may never find them. They may already be on the Planet Liron!"

9

Gone

"Keep looking," Melody said. "I'm not going to give up yet."

"Let's look down here," Howie suggested.

Melody followed Howie down the dark hallway. A huge claw hung on one side of the hall and Melody squeezed against the other side to stay away from it. Big hats and a sword barely showed in the light from the exit sign. Howie had to jump to avoid a hook that nearly grabbed his shirt.

"What kind of crazy place is this?" Melody muttered. "A kid could get hurt around here."

"I'm afraid that's exactly what Mr. Spark had in mind," Howie said. "Look at that."

Directly in front of the kids, at the end of the hall, stood a huge black bowl. It was completely empty but had strange switches on the side.

"If it wasn't for the switches," said Melody, "this bowl would look like a witch's cauldron."

"I have a bad feeling about this," Howie whispered. "Let's . . ." A low moaning sound stopped Howie from finishing his sentence.

"What in the world was that?" Melody said as the moaning grew louder and louder.

Howie gulped. "It sounds like Eddie."

"He must be hurt," Melody squealed. "We have to find him. Fast!" Melody grabbed a door handle beside the big bowl and pulled. It opened with a loud *screeeeech*.

It took Howie and Melody a minute to adjust their eyes to the bright lights of the room. Standing with their backs to them were Liza and Eddie.

Melody stomped her foot. "Liza and Eddie! You scared us to death! Why did you run off like that?"

Liza and Eddie didn't say a word; they just stared at something in a corner. Howie grabbed Eddie's arm and started to yell at him, but he stopped short when he saw what Liza and Eddie were staring at.

"What is that?" Melody asked.

"What does it look like?" Eddie grumbled. "Mr. Sparks ate all the candy and he didn't even save one teeny bit for us!"

Melody had to admit it looked bad. A huge mountain of empty candy bags stood in the corner of the little room.

"Maybe there's a little left," Howie suggested.

Liza shook her head sadly. "No, we checked every single bag. They're as empty as the candy shelves at the store."

"Maybe it's for the party," Howie said, but he didn't sound very sure.

51

"No," Eddie said. "We've been through all the storage rooms and there wasn't any candy. It's gone . . . all gone."

Liza nodded. "There isn't any candy," she said. "Aliens have stolen it!"

10

Sugar-Free

"I bet Mr. Spark is from Toledo. He's no alien — he's just a candy hog! He took my chocolate!" Eddie kicked the empty candy bags and sent three flying into the air.

"I'll prove that Mr. Spark is an alien," Liza told Melody, Howie, and Eddie.

"How can you do that?" Melody asked Liza.

"Come on," Liza said. "Let's get out of here and I'll show you." Liza didn't say another word. She led her friends out the back gym door and into the parking lot of Bailey Elementary.

"Will you please tell us where we're going?" Howie asked.

Liza put a finger to her lips and kept

walking. Liza led them to a small gas station.

"Oh, no," Eddie said. "Fill us up with regular."

Melody giggled at Eddie. "Just as long as it's not sugar-free!"

Liza went straight to the candy counter inside the gas station. No candy.

"This is very strange," Howie said.

"Come on," Liza said. She ran to Dover's Five and Dime store on Main Street. Every aisle was filled with toys and clothing, but when the kids turned to the candy aisle they saw nothing. It was totally empty.

"This is the worst thing to ever happen to Bailey City," Eddie moaned. "How could anyone be so cruel?"

"Wait," Liza said. She ran out the door.

"Where is she going now?" Howie asked.

"We better follow her and find out," Melody said.

Eddie groaned. "Candy. I need candy."

Melody rolled her eyes and pulled Eddie out of the store.

"Which way did she go?" Howie asked.

"Don't tell me she's disappeared again," Melody said.

Eddie saw a yellow scarf slip around the corner of Green Street. "There she goes," Eddie said. The kids followed Liza into Bloom's Food, the biggest grocery store in Bailey City.

"All right," Eddie said, zipping around Liza. "This store is bound to have candy left. They have more stuff than anywhere else."

Eddie's sneakers squeaked to a halt at the beginning of aisle six. He couldn't believe his eyes. The four kids stared in silence down the long row. No candy. Every shelf was completely bare.

Howie grabbed a grocery clerk as she walked by with a mop. "Hey, what happened to all the candy?" Howie asked her.

The lady shrugged. "Some guy came in

here the other day and bought everything we had, even the licorice sticks."

Liza folded her arms over her chest. "Was that man short and wearing shiny pants?"

"Why, yes," the lady said. "How did you know?"

"It was a lucky guess," Liza said as the lady walked away.

Liza faced her friends and pointed to the empty shelves. "Now do you believe me?" she asked. "Mr. Spark is an alien who has come to Earth to find an energy source. Candy. If we don't do something about it, you can say good-bye to chocolate and jelly beans and jawbreakers forever."

11

Third-Grade Blob

Eddie plopped down right in the middle of aisle six. "Life without chocolate? Without gumdrops? Without lollipops? It's . . . it's . . . it's . . ."

"Unthinkable!" Howie said, his stomach rumbling with hunger for candy.

"But what can we do about it?" Melody asked. "Eventually, the stores will get in more candy."

"How long will that take?" Eddie moaned. He fell backward onto the floor and rolled around like he was in pain.

"The problem is that Mr. Spark might buy it all up again," Liza said softly.

Eddie sat up. "We have to stop him."

Liza looked at the empty shelves and her eyes got big. "I do have an idea," she said. "But you're not going to like it."

Eddie jumped up from the floor and grabbed Liza's arm. "Tell me," he said. "I'll do anything!"

"Anything?" Liza asked.

"You mean you'll actually work?" Melody asked Eddie.

Howie put his hand on Eddie's shoulder. "We all have to work together to save Bailey City from the aliens."

"Some things, like candy, are worth working for," Eddie said seriously. "Tell me your plan. I'm ready to help."

Liza bent her head down and whispered her idea. She was right. Eddie didn't like the plan, but he did agree to follow it.

"Meet back here in an hour," Liza told her friends, "and bring reinforcements."

Liza, Melody, Howie, and Eddie scattered. In exactly one hour, they returned with a few other kids.

"What's this all about?" a kid named Patrick asked.

A pretty girl named Becky shrugged.

"I don't know, but if it helps us get candy for Halloween I'll try anything."

Patrick and the other kids nodded. They walked around the store with Liza, Melody, Howie, and Eddie. Soon, their arms were loaded with supplies.

"Do you really think this will work?" Howie asked his friends.

"It has to," Eddie said. "I can't go through life without candy. I'd shrivel up and be a third-grade blob."

Melody giggled. "All right, Mr. Blob. Let's head over to my house and get ready to kick some alien behind."

12

Choco-line

"This is it," Melody said. "Party day."

"I hope this works," Howie said. The four kids were in Melody's kitchen. It was Saturday and they were dressed in their costumes. Eddie had already stuck Melody twice with his Viking horns and Howie had accidentally swung his cowboy hat into Liza's face. Liza was so nervous she kept turning the light in her Statue of Liberty torch on and off. Melody squeezed her laser gun tight and wondered if Mr. Spark had a real laser that worked on kids.

"We're as ready as we'll ever be," Liza said with a big sigh. "Let's go."

"Roar!" Eddie yelled, beating his chest. "Me Viking! Me scare alien!"

The four kids grabbed their treat bags

and headed to Bailey Elementary. "Mr. Spark could be gone," Howie suggested as they walked down the sidewalk. "Maybe he got all the candy he needs and blasted off before the party."

Melody smiled, hoping Howie was right. After all, they had met other adults that they thought were aliens and everything had turned out fine. The Halloween party would probably be fine, too. Wouldn't it?

"No such luck," Eddie groaned as Mr. Spark greeted a line of kids at the door.

"Welcome," Mr. Spark squeaked with a big smile. "Please put your candy in here." Mr. Spark pointed to the huge black bowl the kids had seen backstage.

"I bet that's what he uses to convert the candy into energy for his spaceship," Liza whispered. "He uses candy like gasoline."

"That would make my favorite candy bar choco-line," Eddie said in an angry voice. "This madman must be stopped." Eddie pushed his way to the front of the group.

"Before you enter," Mr. Spark said with a smile that didn't look friendly at all, "you must donate one bag of treats for the party."

"Gladly," Eddie said with an equally unfriendly smile. He reached into his treat sack and pulled out a plastic bag to hand to Mr. Spark. Mr. Spark looked at

what was in the bag. His eyes grew as round as saucers and he held the bag with his fingertips as far away from himself as he could.

"What is this?" Mr. Spark screeched.

Eddie grinned even more. "Those," he said, "are CARROTS!"

Melody stepped up next. "And I brought APPLES," she told Mr. Spark. Soon, lots of kids were shoving bags full of healthy treats toward Mr. Spark.

"We have no candy," Howie said. "We brought fruit and vegetables."

"That's right," Liza said. "All the candy is gone. There's nothing left."

"NOOOOOO!" Mr. Spark yelled. "You've ruined everything!"

13

Huge Problem

Suddenly, the lights dimmed and music began. "The party is starting," the boy named Patrick yelled. Patrick and a crowd of kids pushed through the door.

Liza, Melody, Howie, and Eddie huddled together near the punch bowl. "Do you think our plan worked?" Liza asked.

Melody shrugged. "I don't see Mr. Spark anymore. Maybe we scared him off." Kids danced and showed off their costumes throughout the gym, but Melody couldn't see Mr. Spark's shiny pants anywhere.

A loud roaring noise rumbled through the gym, shaking the wooden floor. "They need to turn that music down," Howie yelled.

Eddie shook his head. "That isn't music. That's Mr. Spark taking off!"

Liza's eyes got wide. "Let's go check."

The kids looked backstage for Mr. Spark. He was nowhere to be found. The storage rooms were empty. Every control panel had disappeared. Even the huge green blob was gone.

"This is wonderful," Liza squealed. "We saved Bailey City from aliens!"

Melody laughed. "Did you see the look on Mr. Spark's face when Eddie held up those carrots? I bet Mr. Spark left this planet and will never come back."

Eddie had a glum look on his face.

"What's wrong?" Howie asked Eddie. "You should be happy — we saved the Earth."

"I am," Eddie admitted. "But we still have a huge problem."

"We do?" Liza asked.

Eddie nodded sadly. "We only have healthy snacks for treats."

Melody laughed. "Maybe aliens from planet Liron aren't the only ones who need candy for fuel."

Liza smiled at Eddie. "I may know how to get rid of aliens, but I can also read a cookbook."

"What are you talking about?" Eddie asked.

Liza pulled a big wad of tinfoil from her treat bag. Wrapped inside was home-made chocolate fudge.

"Liza," Eddie said seriously as he grabbed a handful of chocolate, "today, you truly did save Bailey City!"

Out-of-this-
world Puzzles
and Activities

Creepy Crossword Puzzle

Now that you've read *Aliens Don't Carve Jack-o'-lanterns,* can you answer the questions in this puzzle?

Across
1. Who is the first Bailey School kid to think that Mr. Spark is an alien?
2. The kids think Mr. Spark is from outer_____.
3. What does Melody use to make her hair stand up like antennae?
4. Where in the school is the Halloween party held?

Down
4. What does Mr. Spark tell the kids they will play at the party?
5. What treat does Melody bring to the Halloween party?
6. What does Howie dress up as for Halloween?

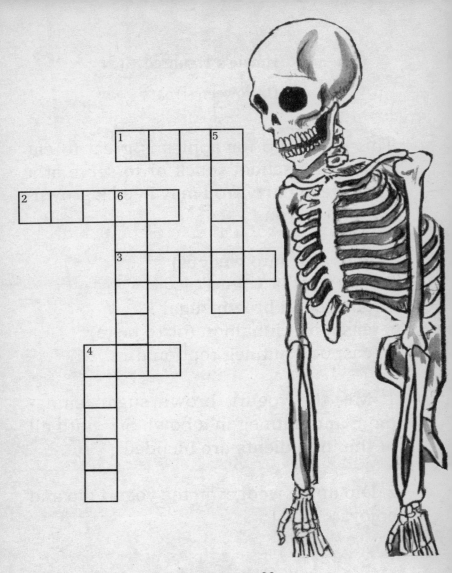

Answers on page 88.

Howie's Haunted Halloween Treats

This quick dip for apples is great to eat as an after-school snack or to serve at a Halloween party. You may need a grown-up to help you.

Apples (cut into wedges)
2 cups vanilla yogurt
1 tablespoon brown sugar
½ teaspoon cinnamon (or to taste)
¼ teaspoon nutmeg (optional)

1. Mix the yogurt, brown sugar, cinnamon, and nutmeg in a bowl. Stir until all of the ingredients are blended.

2. Dip apple wedges in the yogurt dip and enjoy!

Wacky Word Search

Can you find the words hidden below? They can be horizontal, vertical, diagonal, and even backward.

Words: CHOCOLATE, ALIEN, CANDY, PARTY, PLANET, TRICK, TREATS

```
G C T R I C K
Q H A L I E N
R O C N B Z I
S C T M D J S
V O R A V Y X
P L S R Z W U
P A R T Y O Q
W T R E A T S
A E P I W O Z
I T E N A L P
```

Answers on page 88.

Write your own Bailey School Kids adventure! On the following pages is a scene taken from *Aliens Don't Carve Jack-o'-lanterns* — but some words are missing.

Before you even look at the passage, fill in the following blanks. Try to choose words that are silly, funny, spooky, or weird. When you are done, copy the words in order into the blank spaces on pages 80–81. Then read your brand-new BSK scene to your friends and family!

Adjective: _____Alien_____

Plural noun: _____aliens_____

Plural noun: _____dog_____

Adjective: _____silly_____

Plural noun: _Monkeys_

Your name: _Shayna_

Name of a friend: _Catie_

Adjective: _funny_

Noun: _Pizza Hut_

Adjective: _excited_

Your name: _Shayna_

Same friend's name: _Cate_

Adjective: _surprised_

Number: _1000_

Same friend's name: _Catie_

Name of a famous
person: _Britney Spears_

79

The kids tiptoed down the (_____)
                                                    adjective

hallway. Even though they were trying

to be quiet, their (_____)
                                        plural noun

echoed like (_____). (_____)
                    plural noun   adjective

(_____) from old plays hung on the
      plural noun

walls of the hallway. (_____)
                                        your name

and (_____) passed
              your friend's name

(_____) masks, a king's
          adjective

(_____), and (_____) trees.
      noun   adjective

(_____) grabbed
              your name

(_____) when a (_____)
      same friend's name   adjective

skeleton swung out in front of them.

"If we don't find them in (_____)
number

minutes," (_____) said with a
same friend's name

shudder, "I'm getting out of here and

telling (_____)!"
name of a famous person

Make Your Own Alien Pumpkin

You may need an adult to help you with this project.

You will need:
Small pumpkin or gourd
Poster paint (tempera and acrylics also work) or markers
Brushes
Pipe cleaners
Poster putty
Construction paper
Newspaper
Optional items: Glitter, yarn, leaves, stickers, old party hats, streamers

Before you begin, place sheets of old newspaper on your workspace to make cleaning up fast and easy.

For the Funny Face:

You can make a stencil out of construction paper for your alien pumpkin's eyes. Here are some shapes that Mr. Spark used for his jack-o'-lanterns.

- Trace the shapes onto a piece of construction paper and cut them out.

- Then hold the stencil against the pumpkin.

- Paint over the shape and pull the paper away. Be careful not to smudge the eye. Hold the stencil in all different positions to make the eyes look wacky and weird.

- Invent your own out-of-this-world shapes for the mouth, nose, and ears. You can make stencils or paint the features on freehand.

For the Alien Antennae:

- Twist or bend the pipe cleaners to create alien antennae. Make them any shape, size, or style you'd like.

- Stick a thick wad of poster putty on your pumpkin wherever you want to attach an antenna.

- Then push the bottom of the pipe cleaner into the wad of poster putty. You can also wrap the pipe cleaners around the pumpkin's stem.

Spacey Extras:

Be creative! Paint your pumpkin's face green, glue glitter onto your pumpkin to make it sparkle, add creepy Halloween stickers, or give your pumpkin hair.

Liza's No-bake Chocolate Cookies

You may need an adult to help you with this recipe.

You will need:

2 cups sugar
$\frac{1}{4}$ cup cocoa
$\frac{1}{2}$ cup milk
$\frac{1}{4}$ cup margarine
1 teaspoon vanilla
1 pinch salt
$\frac{1}{2}$ cup chunky peanut butter
3 cups quick cooking oatmeal

1. Mix the sugar, milk, cocoa, and margarine in a pot.

2. Cook the mixture on medium heat until it boils.

3. Remove the pot from the heat and let it cool for one minute.

4. Add vanilla, peanut butter, salt, and oatmeal. Stir well.

5. Drop by teaspoon onto wax paper.

Enjoy this Halloween treat!

Answer Key

Wacky Word Search
page 77

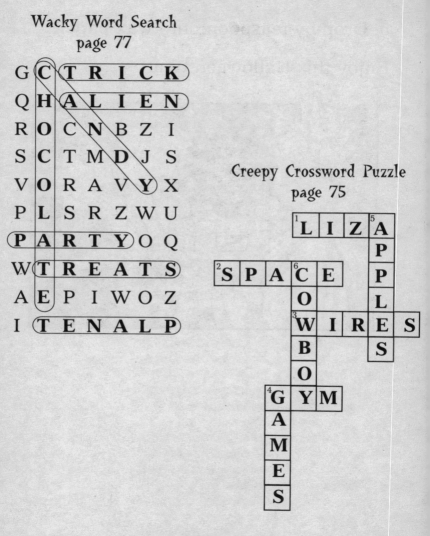

Creepy Crossword Puzzle
page 75

Creepy, weird, wacky, and funny things happen to the Bailey School Kids!™ Collect and read them all!